STAR WARS REBELS™

EZRA
AND THE PILOT

ADAPTED BY JENNIFER HEDDLE

BASED ON THE EPISODE
"PROPERTY OF EZRA BRIDGER,"
WRITTEN BY SIMON KINBERG

DISNEY
LUCASFILM
PRESS

LOS ANGELES • NEW YORK

Printed in the United States of America

First Edition 10 9 8 7 6 5 4 3 2

Library of Congress Control Number: 2014937128

G658-7729-4-14303

ISBN 978-1-4847-0486-8

Visit www.starwars.com

SUSTAINABLE
FORESTRY
INITIATIVE

Certified Chain of Custody
Promoting Sustainable Forestry

www.sfiprogram.org
SFI-01415

The SFI label applies to the text stock

Meet Ezra.

Ezra is fourteen years old.

He lives on the planet Lothal.

Ezra lives in an empty tower
outside the city.

He lives alone,
but that is fine with Ezra.

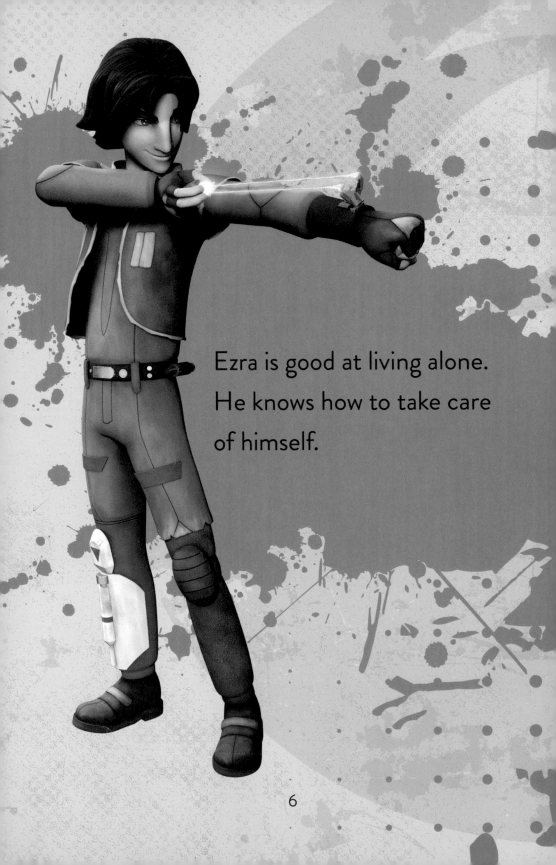

Ezra is good at living alone.
He knows how to take care
of himself.

Lothal is under control of the Empire.
Ezra doesn't like the Empire.
He thinks the people of Lothal
should be free.

One day Ezra was out walking.

He heard a loud sound and
looked up.

He saw a TIE fighter
chasing a starship through the sky.

The TIE fighter was from the Empire.
The starship fired at the TIE fighter.

The TIE fighter fell out of the sky
and crashed not far away.
Ezra didn't like the TIE fighter.

Ezra ran to the crashed TIE fighter.

He pounded on the window of the ship.

Ezra climbed onto the ship
and tried to pull open the hatch.
It was stuck.
The pilot couldn't get out.

Ezra pulled and pulled
until the hatch opened!

Ezra saw the pilot inside.
The pilot was from the Empire.

He was very angry.

He told Ezra to get off his ship.

The pilot did not even say
thank you to Ezra for helping him.
Ezra thought that was rude.

The pilot did not want Ezra's help.
He thought he was better
than Ezra.

Ezra had a plan.

He would teach the pilot a lesson.

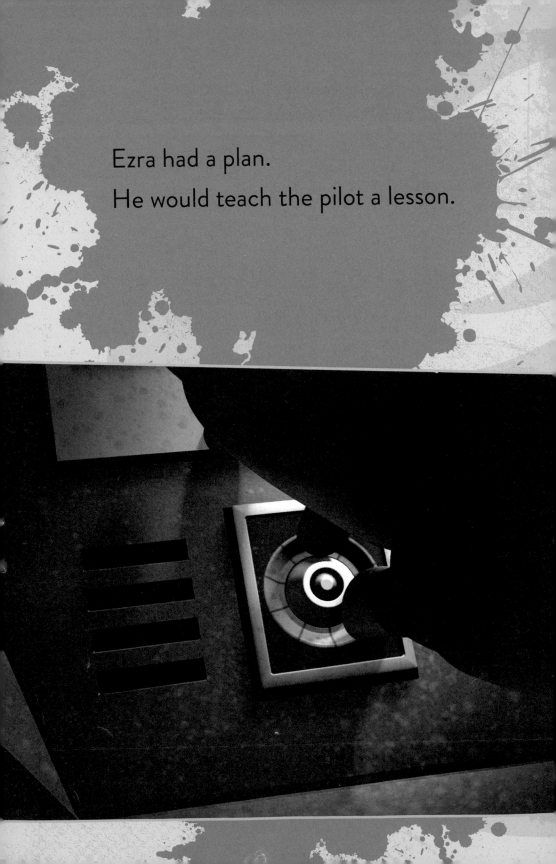

Ezra decided to take parts
from the broken ship.

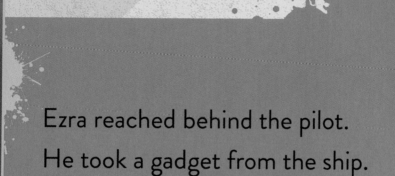

Ezra reached behind the pilot.
He took a gadget from the ship.
The pilot didn't see.

Then Ezra grabbed the pilot's helmet
and jumped off the ship!

The pilot realized what Ezra had done and became even angrier.

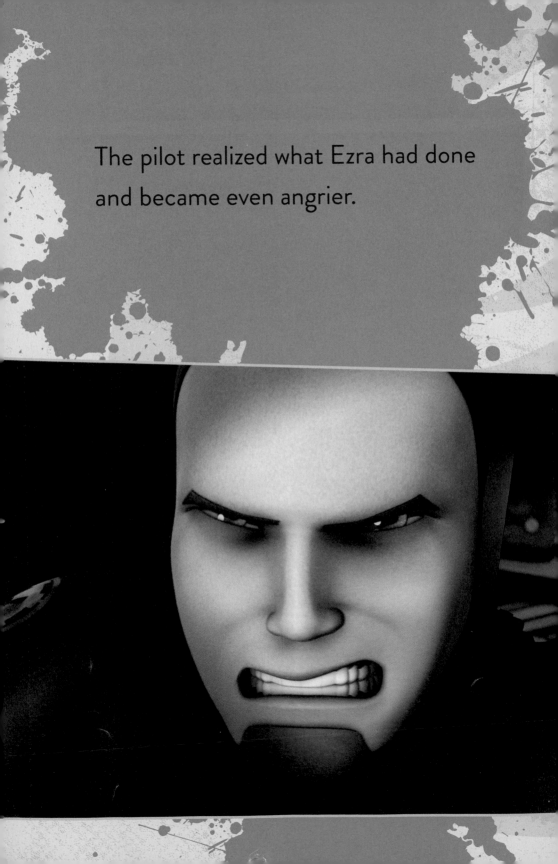

He turned on the ship's cannons!

The cannons fired. *Boom!*
But Ezra was too quick.
He jumped out of the way.
The pilot was surprised.

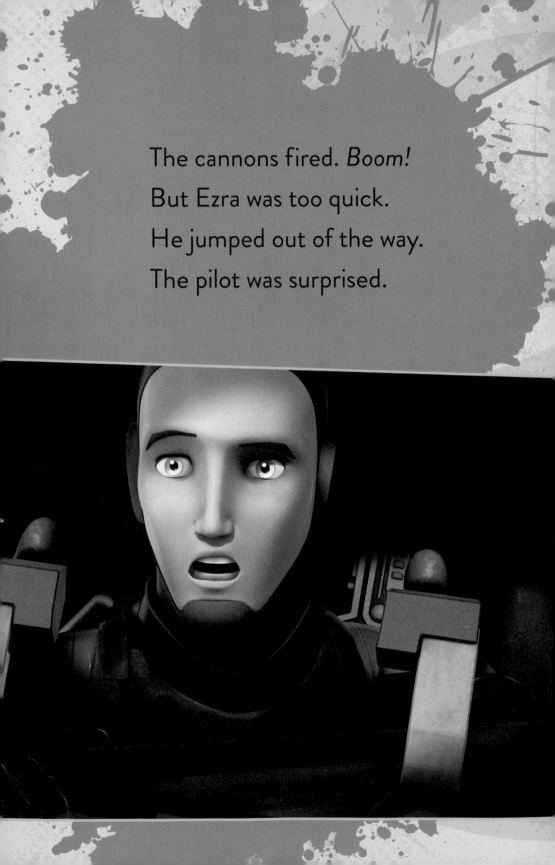

Ezra took out his special slingshot.
He fired it at the TIE fighter.

Ezra's shot bounced off the ship
and hit the pilot in the head!

The pilot was knocked out!

Ezra smiled.

He picked up the pilot's helmet.

It belonged to Ezra now.

Ezra put on the helmet.
It was too big for him,
but that was fine with Ezra.
He liked it anyway.

Ezra saluted and
said thanks to the pilot.
But he still didn't like the Empire.